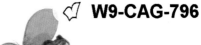

Little Panda

Written and illustrated by Renata Liwska

sandpiper

Houghton Mifflin Harcourt
Boston   New York

Just the other day, Grandfather Panda was talking to his grandson.

"I am going to tell you a story of a little panda and the tiger that flew," he said.

"But that's silly. Tigers can't fly," interrupted the grandchild.

"How do you know if you haven't heard the story yet?" asked Grandfather.

"Once there was a little panda named Bao Bao," Grandfather began.

"He lived with his mother, Lin Lin, in the misty mountains. They lived alone, but Bao Bao did not feel alone. He had his mother, and she was the world to him."

"Here I come, Mama!" Bao Bao hollered as he ran and chased his mother.

"I've got you now!" he yelled as they wrestled.

"Up here!" he laughed as they climbed and swung from the branches.

"Down here!" he shouted as he fell from the trees.

(Bao Bao was very good at falling.)

Playing was not just for fun.

It was also the way Lin Lin taught Bao Bao important

panda lessons.

"Run if someone chases you," his mother advised.

"Wrestle with them if they get too close, and most

important—climb a big tree to get away."

After playtime, his mother sat down to snack on her
favorite food, bamboo.
Lin Lin loved to eat almost as much as Bao Bao
loved to play—which was good, because grown-up
pandas have to eat a lot of bamboo.

So much, in fact, that Bao Bao's mother sometimes needed
to travel for hours, if not days, in search of food.

But the little panda did not mind. If there was one thing he liked more than playing, it was sleeping. When his mother went in search of bamboo, he climbed up his favorite tree to nap until she returned.

One day, Lin Lin said to Bao Bao, "Don't you think
you are getting too big for that little tree?"
"Of course not. It's my favorite spot!" he answered.
"Well, you be careful while I am gone," warned his
mother as she left in search of food.

But Bao Bao did not hear her. He was already asleep.

Every now and then Bao Bao would wake to stretch his
legs or readjust his position before going back to sleep.
Once, as he was moving to get comfortable, he heard
a noise from below.

Thinking it was his mother, he called down sleepily,
"Mama, is that you back from your bamboo dinner?"

But his mother did not answer. Instead, a deep voice
purred, "I had something else in mind for dinner."

Bao Bao scurried higher up the tree.

The tiger followed, and scratched him on the bottom.

"OUCH!" he cried.

Bao Bao climbed higher still, but it was such a small tree. Soon he reached the top and couldn't go any farther. The tiger lunged. "I have you now!" he growled.

But the tiger missed . . .

Bao Bao fell just as the cat struck (he was very good at falling). When Bao Bao looked up, he saw that the tree was empty and the tiger was nowhere in sight.

A little while later, his mother returned.

"I just saw the strangest thing: a tiger flying through the sky," she said.

"That's silly. Tigers can't fly!" Bao Bao answered from his perch high above on a very large tree.

"And that's my story," Grandfather said. "What do you think?"

"Well . . . if you put it that way, I guess a tiger could have flown," the grandchild admitted.

"I guess you'll just have to take my word for it," Grandfather said.

For Michael,

Without whom this book would not be.

Thank you for your love and support.

SANDPIPER and the SANDPIPER logo are trademarks of Houghton
Mifflin Harcourt Publishing Company.

For information about permission to reproduce selections from this book, write to
Permissions, Houghton Mifflin Harcourt Publishing Company,
215 Park Avenue South, New York, New York 10003.

www.hmhbooks.com

The text of this book is set in Humanist and Avenir.
The illustrations are drawn with pencil and colored digitally.

The Library of Congress has cataloged the hardcover edition as follows:

Liwska, Renata.
The little panda / written and illustrated by Renata Liwska.
p. cm.
Summary: A grandfather tells his grandson an unlikely story about a panda
and how it escapes from the tiger that wants to eat it.
[1. Pandas—Fiction.] I. Title.
PZ7.L7652Li 2008
[E]—dc22
2007047735

ISBN 978-0-618-96627-1 hardcover
ISBN 978-0-547-57684-8 paperback

Manufactured in Singapore
TWP 10 9 8 7 6 5 4 3 2 1

4500323616